J. H. Stellar
1927

THE
WORLD'S
ONE HUNDRED
BEST SHORT STORIES

VOLUME EIGHT
M E N

THE
WORLD'S
ONE HUNDRED
BEST SHORT STORIES

[IN TEN VOLUMES]

GRANT OVERTON
EDITOR - IN - CHIEF

VOLUME EIGHT
MEN

FUNK & WAGNALLS COMPANY
NEW YORK and LONDON

CONTENTS

THE WORLD'S 100 BEST SHORT STORIES

WORDS AND MUSIC

By Irvin S. Cobb

When Breck Tandy killed a man he made a number of mistakes. In the first place, he killed the most popular man in Forked Deer County—the county clerk, a man named Abner J. Rankin. In the second place, he killed him with no witnesses present, so that it stood his word—and he a newcomer and a stranger—against the mute, eloquent accusation of a riddled dead man. And in the third place, he sent north of the Ohio River for a lawyer to defend him.

.   .   .   .

On the first Monday in June—Court Monday—the town filled up early. Before the field larks were out of the grass the farmers were tying their teams to the gnawed hick-racks along the square. By nine o'clock the swapping ring below the wagonyard was swimming in red dust and clamorous with the chaffer of the horse-traders. In front of a vacant store the Ladies' Aid Society of Zion Baptist Church had a canvas sign out, announcing that an elegant dinner would be served for twenty-five cents from twelve to one, also ice cream and cake all day for fifteen cents.

The narrow wooden sidewalks began to creak and churn under the tread of many feet. A long-haired medicine doctor emerged from his frock-coat like a locust coming out of its shell, pushed his high hat off his forehead and ranged a guitar, sundry bottles of a potent mixture, his tooth-pulling forceps, and a trick-handkerchief upon the narrow shelf of his stand alongside the Drummers' Home Hotel. In front of the little dingy tent of the Half Man and Half Horse a yellow negro sat on a split-bottom chair limbering up for a hard day. This yellow negro was an artist. He played a common twenty-cent mouth organ, using his left hand to slide it back and forth across his spread lips. The other hand held a pair of polished beef bones, such as end men wield, and about the wrist was buckled a broad leather strap with three big sleigh-bells riveted loosely to the leather, so that he could clap the bones and shake the bells with the same motion. He was a whole orchestra in himself. He could play on his mouth organ almost any tune you wanted, and with his bones and his bells to help out he could creditably imitate a church organ, a fife-and-drum corps, or, indeed, a full brass band. He had his chair tilted back until his woolly head dented a draggled banner depicting in five faded primary colors the physical attractions of the Half Man and Half Horse—Marvel of the Century—and he tested his mouth organ with short, mellow, tentative blasts as he waited until the Marvel and the Marvel's manager finished a belated breakfast within and the first ballyhoo could start. He was practising the newest of the ragtime airs to get that far South. The name of it was The Georgia Camp-Meeting.

The town marshal in his shirt sleeves, with a big

silver shield pinned to the breast of his unbuttoned blue waistcoat and hickory stick with a crook handle for added emblem of authority, stalked the town drunkard, fair game at all seasons and especially on Court Monday. The town gallant whirled back and forth the short hilly length of Main Street in his new side-bar buggy. A clustering group of negroes made a thick, black blob, like hiving bees, in front of a negro fishhouse, from which came the smell and sounds of perch and channel cat frying on spitting-hot skillets. High up on the squat cupola of the courthouse a red-headed woodpecker clung, barred in crimson, white, and blue-black, like a bit of living bunting, engaged in the hopeless task of trying to drill through the tin sheathing. The rolling rattle of his beak's tattoo came down sharply to the crowd below. Mourning doves called to one another in the trees round the red-brick courthouse, and at ten o'clock, when the sun was high and hot, the sheriff came out and, standing be-tween two hollow white pillars, rapped upon one of them with a stick and called upon all witnesses and talesmen to come into court for the trial of John Breckinridge Tandy, charged with murder in the first degree, against the peace and dignity of the common-wealth of Tennessee and the statutes made and pro-vided.

But this ceremonial by the sheriff was for form rather than effect, since the witnesses and the talesmen all sat in the circuit-court chamber along with as many of the population of Forked Deer County as could squeeze in there. Already the air of the crowded cham-ber was choky with heat and rancid with smell. Men were perched precariously in the ledges of the win-dows. More men were ranged in rows along the

plastered walls, clunking their heels against the cracked
wooden baseboards. The two front rows of benches
were full of women. For this was to be the big case
of the June term—a better show by long odds than
the Half Man and Half Horse.

Inside the low railing that divided the room and on
the side nearer the jury box were the forces of the
defense. Under his skin the prisoner showed a sallow
paleness born of his three months in the county jail.
He was tall and dark and steady eyed, a young man,
well under thirty. He gave no heed to those who sat
in packed rows behind him, wishing him evil. He kept
his head turned front, only bending it sometimes to
whisper with one of his lawyers or one of his witnesses.
Frequently, tho, his hand went out in a protecting,
reassuring way to touch his wife's brown hair or to
rest a moment on her small shoulder. She was a plain,
scared, shrinking little thing. The fingers of her thin
hand were plaited desperately together in her lap.
Already she was trembling. Once in a while she would
raise her face, showing shallow brown eyes dilated with
fright, and then sink her head again like a quail trying
to hide. She looked pitiable and lonely.

The chief attorney for the defense was half turned
from the small counsel table where he might study the
faces of the crowd. He was from Middle Indiana,
serving his second term in Congress. If his party held
control of the state he would go to the Senate after
the next election. He was an orator of parts and a
pleader of almost a national reputation. He had manly
grace and he was a fine, upstanding figure of a man,
and before now he had wrung victories out of many dif-
ficult cases. But he chilled to his finger-nails with

apprehensions of disaster as he glanced searchingly about the close-packed room.

Wherever he looked he saw no friendliness at all. He could feel the hostility of that crowd as tho it had substance and body. It was a tangible thing; it was almost a physical thing. Why, you could almost put your hand out and touch it. It was everywhere there.

And it focussed and was summed up in the person of Aunt Tilly Haslett, rearing on the very front bench with her husband, Uncle Fayette, half hidden behind her vast and overflowing bulk. Aunt Tilly made public opinion in Hyattsville. Indeed she was public opinion in that town. In her it had its up-comings and its out-flowings. She held herself bolt upright, filling out the front of her black bombazine basque until the buttons down its front strained at their buttonholes. With wide, deliberate strokes she fanned herself with a palm-leaf fan. The fan had an edging of black tape sewed round it—black tape signifying in that community age or mourning, or both. Her jaw was set like a steel latch, and her little gray eyes behind her steel-bowed specs were leveled with a baleful, condemning glare that included the strange lawyer, his client, his client's wife, and all that was his client's.

Congressman Durham looked and knew that his presence was an affront to Aunt Tilly and all those who sat with her; that his somewhat vivid tie, his silken shirt, his low tan shoes, his new suit of gray flannels—a masterpiece of the best tailor in Indianapolis—were as insults, added up and piled on, to this suspendered, gingham-shirted constituency. Better than ever he realized now the stark hopelessness of the task to which his hands were set. And he dreaded what was coming almost as much for himself as for the man he was hired to defend. But he was a trained veteran of courtroom campaigns, and there was a jauntily assumed confidence in his bearing as he swung himself about and made a brisk show of conferring with the local attorney who was to aid him in the choosing of the jurors and the questioning of the witnesses.

But it was real confidence and real jauntiness that radiated from the other wing of the inclosure, where the prosecutor sat with the assembled bar of Forked Deer County on his flanks, volunteers upon the favored side, lending to it the moral support of weight and numbers. Rankin, the dead man, having been a bachelor, State's Attorney Gilliam could bring no lorn widow and children to mourn before the jurors' eyes and win added sympathy for his cause. Lacking these most valued assets of a murder trial he supplied their places with the sisters of the dead man—two sparse-built elderly women in heavy black, with sweltering thick veils down over their faces. When the proper time came he would have them raise these veils and show their woeful faces, but now they sat shrouded all in crepe, fit figures of desolation and sorrow. He fussed about busily, fiddling the quill toothpick that hung perilously in the corner of his mouth and evening up the edges of a pile of law books with freckled calfskin covers. He was a lank, bony garfish of a man, with a white goatee aggressively protruding from his lower lip. He was a poor speaker but mighty as a cross-examiner, and he was serving his first term and was a candidate for another. He wore the official garbing of special and extraordinary occasions—long black coat and limp white waistcoat and gray striped trousers, a trifle short in the legs.

He felt the importance of his place here almost visibly—his figure swelled and expanded out his clothes.

"Look yonder at Tom Gilliam," said Mr. Lukins, the grocer, in tones of whispered admiration to his next-elbow neighbor, "just prunin' and honin' hisse'f to git at that there Tandy and his dude Yankee lawyer. If he don't chaw both of 'em up together I'll be dad-burned."

"You bet," whispered back his neighbor—it was Aunt Tilly's oldest son, Fayette, Junior—"it's like Maw says—time's come to teach them murderin' Kintuckians they can't be a-comin' down here a-killin' up people and not pay for it. I reckon, Mr. Lukins," added Fayette, Junior, with a wriggle of pleased anticipation, "we shore are goin' to see some carryin's-on in this cotehouse today."

Mr. Lukins' reply was lost to history because just then the judge entered—an elderly, kindly-looking man—from his chambers in the rear, with the circuit-court clerk right behind him bearing large leather-clad books and sheaves of foolscap paper. Their coming made a bustle. Aunt Tilly squared herself forward, scrooging Uncle Fayette yet farther into the eclipse of her shapeless figure. The prisoner raised his head and eyed his judge. His wife looked only at the interlaced, weaving fingers in her lap.

The formalities of the opening of a term of court were mighty soon over; there was everywhere manifest a haste to get at the big thing. The clerk called the case of the Commonwealth versus Tandy. Both sides were ready. Through the local lawyer, delegated for these smaller purposes, the accused man pleaded not guilty. The clerk spun the jury wheel, which was a painted wooden drum on a creaking wooden axle, and drew forth a slip of paper with the name of a talesman written upon it and read aloud:

"Isom W. Tolliver."

In an hour the jury was complete: two townsmen, a clerk and a telegraph operator, and ten men from the country—farmers mainly and one blacksmith and one horse-trader. Three of the panel who owned up frankly to a fixed bias had been let go by consent of both sides. Three more were sure they could give the defendant a fair trial, but those three the local lawyer had challenged peremptorily. The others were accepted as they came. The foreman was a brownskinned, sparrow-hawk-looking old man, with a smoldering brown eye. He had spare, knotted hands, like talons, and the right one was marred and twisted, with a sprayed bluish scar in the midst of the crippled knuckles like the mark of an old gunshot wound. Juror No. 4 was a stodgy old man, a small planter from the back part of the county, who fanned himself steadily with a brown-varnished straw hat. No. 7 was even older, a white-whiskered patriarch on crutches. The twelfth jury-man was the oldest of the twelve—he looked to be almost seventy, but he went into the box after he had sworn that his sight and hearing and general health were good and that he still could do his ten hours a day at his blacksmith shop. This juryman chewed tobacco without pause. Twice after he took his seat at the back end of the double line he tried for a wooden cuspidor ten feet away. Both were creditable attempts, but he missed each time. Seeing the look of gathering distress in his eyes the sheriff brought the cuspidor nearer, and thereafter No. 12 was content, chewing steadily like some bearded contemplative ruminant and listening attentively to the evidence, meanwhile scratching a very wiry head of white-red hair with a thumb-nail that through some injury had taken on the appearance of a very thick, very black Brazil nut. This scratching made a raspy, filing sound that after a while got on Congressman Durham's nerves.

It was late in the afternoon when the prosecution rested its case and court adjourned until the following morning. The state's attorney had not had so very much evidence to offer, really—the testimony of one who heard the single shot and ran in at Rankin's door to find Rankin upon the floor, about dead, with a pistol, unfired, in his hand and Tandy standing against the wall with a pistol, fired, in his hand; the constable to whom Tandy surrendered; the physician who examined the body; the persons who knew of the quarrel between Tandy and Rankin growing out of a land deal into which they had gone partners—not much, but enough for Gilliam's purposes. Once in the midst of examining a witness the state's attorney, seemingly by accident, let his look fall upon the two black-robed, silent figures at his side, and as tho overcome by the sudden realization of a great grief, he faltered and stopped dead and sank down. It was an old trick, but well done, and a little humming murmur like a breeze coming through treetops swept the audience.

Durham was sick in his soul as he came away. In his mind there stood the picture of a little, scared woman's drawn, drenched face. She had started crying before the last juror was chosen and thereafter all day, at half-minute intervals, the big, hard sobs racked her. As Durham came down the steps he had almost to shove his way through a knot of natives outside the doors. They grudged him the path they made for him, and as he showed them his back he heard a snicker and some one said a thing that cut him where he was already bruised—in his egotism. But he gave no heed to the words. What was the use?

At the Drummers' Home Hotel a darky waiter sustained a profound shock when the imported lawyer declined the fried beefsteak with fried potatoes and also the fried ham and eggs. Mastering his surprize the waiter offered to try to get the Northern gentleman a fried pork chop and some fried June apples, but Durham only wanted a glass of milk for his supper. He drank it and smoked a cigar, and about dusk he went upstairs to his room. There he found assembled the forlorn rank and file of the defense, the local lawyer and three character witnesses—prominent citizens from Tandy's home town who were to testify to his good repute in the place where he was born and reared. These would be the only witnesses, except Tandy himself, that Durham meant to call. One of them was a bustling little man named Felsburg, a clothing merchant, and one was Colonel Quigley, a banker and an ex-mayor, and the third was a Judge Priest, who sat on a circuit-court bench back in Kentucky. In contrast to his size, which was considerable, this Judge Priest had a voice that was high and whiny. He also had the trick, common to many men in politics in his part of the South, of being purposely ungrammatical at times.

This mannerism led a lot of people into thinking that the judge must be an uneducated man—until they heard him charging a jury or reading one of his rulings. The judge had other peculiarities. In conversation he nearly always called men younger than himself, son.

He drank a little bit too much sometimes; and nobody had ever beaten him for any office he coveted. Durham didn't know what to make of this old judge— sometimes he seemed simple-minded to the point of childishness almost.

The others were gathered about a table by a lighted kerosene lamp, but the old judge sat at an open window with his low-quarter shoes off and his white-socked feet propped against the ledge. He was industriously stoking at a home-made corncob pipe. He pursed up his mouth, pulling at the long cane stem of his pipe with little audible sucks. From the rocky little street below the clatter of departing farm teams came up to him. The Indian medicine doctor was taking down his big white umbrella and packing up his regalia. The late canvas habitat of the Half Man and Half Horse had been struck and was gone, leaving only the pole-holes in the turf and a trodden space to show where it had stood. Court would go on all week, but Court Monday was over and for another month the town would doze along peacefully.

Durham slumped himself into a chair that screeched protestingly in all its infirm joints. The heart was gone clean out of him.

"I don't understand these people at all," he confessed. "We're beating against a stone wall with our bare hands."

"If it should be money now that you're needing, Mr. Durham," spoke up Felsburg, "that boy Tandy's father was my very good friend when I first walked into that town with a peddling pack on my back, and if it should be money——?"

"It isn't money, Mr. Felsburg," said Durham. "If I didn't get a cent for my services I'd still fight this case out to the end for the sake of that game boy and that poor little mite of a wife of his. It isn't money or the lack of it—it's the damned hate they've built up here against the man. Why, you could cut it off in chunks—the prejudice that there was in that courthouse today."

"Son," put in Judge Priest in his high, weedy voice, "I reckon maybe you're right. I've been projectin' around cotehouses a good many years, and I've taken notice that when a jury look at a prisoner all the time and never look at his women folks it's a monstrous bad sign. And that's the way it was all day today."

"The judge will be fair—he always is," said Hightower, the local lawyer, "and of course Gilliam is only doing his duty. Those jurors are as good solid men as you can find in this country anywhere. But they can't help being prejudiced. Human nature's not strong enough to stand out against the feeling that's grown up round here against Tandy since he shot Ab Rankin."

"Son," said Judge Priest, still with his eyes on the darkening square below, "about how many of them jurors would you say are old soldiers?"

"Four or five that I know of," said Hightower—"and maybe more. It's hard to find a man over fifty years old in this section that didn't see active service in the Big War."

"Ah, hah," assented Judge Priest with a squeaky little grunt. "That foreman now—he looked like he might of seen some fightin'?"

"Four years of it," said Hightower. "He came out a captain in the cavalry."

"Ah, hah." Judge Priest sucked at his pipe.

"Herman," he wheezed back over his shoulder to Felsburg "did you notice a tall sort of a saddle-colored darky playing a juice harp in front of that there side-show as we came along up? I reckon that nigger could play almost any tune you'd a mind to hear him play?"

At a time like this Durham was distinctly not in-terested in the versatilities of strange negroes in this corner of the world. He kept silent, shrugging his shoulders petulantly.

"I wonder now is that nigger left town yet?" mused the old judge half to himself.

"I saw him just a while ago going down toward the depot," volunteered Hightower. "There's a train out of here for Memphis at 8:50. It's about twenty minutes of that now."

"Ah, hah, jest about," assented the judge. When the judge said "Ah, hah!" like that it sounded like the striking of a fiddle-bow across a fiddle's tautened E-string.

"Well, boys," he went on, "we've all got to do the best we can for Breck Tandy, ain't we? Say, son"—this was aimed at Durham—"I'd like mightily for you to put me on the stand the last one tomorrow. You wait until you're through with Herman and Colonel Quigley here, before you call me. And if I should seem to ramble somewhat in giving my testimony—why, son, you just let me ramble, will you? I know these people down here better maybe than you do—and if I should seem inclined to ramble, just let me go ahead and don't stop me, please?"

"Judge Priest," said Durham tartly, "if you think it could possibly do any good, ramble all you like."

"Much obliged," said the old judge, and he struggled into his low-quartered shoes and stood up, dusting the tobacco fluff off himself.

"Herman, have you got any loose change about you?"

Felsburg nodded and reached into his pocket. The judge made a discriminating selection of silver and bills from the handful that the merchant extended to him across the table.

"I'll take about ten dollars," he said. "I didn't come down here with more than enough to jest about buy my railroad ticket and pay my bill at this here tavern, and I might want a sweetenin' dram or somethin'."

He pouched his loan and crossed the room.

"Boys," he said, "I think I'll be knockin' round a little before I turn in. Herman, I may stop by your room a minute as I come back in. You boys better turn in early and git yourselves a good night's sleep. We are all liable to be purty tolerable busy tomorrow."

After he was outside he put his head back in the door and said to Durham:

"Remember, son, I may ramble."

Durham nodded shortly, being somewhat put out by the vagaries of a mind that could concern itself with trivial things on the imminent eve of a crisis.

As the judge creaked ponderously along the hall and down the stairs those he had left behind heard him whistling a tune to himself, making false starts at the air and halting often to correct his meter. It was an unknown tune to them all, but to Felsburg, the oldest of the four, it brought a vague, unplaced memory.

The old judge was whistling when he reached the street. He stood there a minute until he had mastered the tune to his own satisfaction, and then, still whistling, he shuffled along the uneven board pavement, which, after rippling up and down like a broken-backed

snake, dipped downward to a little railroad station at
the foot of the street.

. . . .

In the morning nearly half the town—the white
half—came to the trial, and enough of the black half
to put a dark hem, like a mourning border, across the
back width of the courtroom. Except that Main Street
now drowsed in the heat where yesterday it had buzzed,
this day might have been the day before. Again the
resolute woodpecker drove his bloodied head with un-
impaired energy against the tin sheathing up above.
It was his third summer for that same cupola and the
tin was pocked with little dents for three feet up and
down. The mourning doves still pitched their lament-
ing note back and forth across the courthouse yard;
and in the dewberry patch at the bottom of Aunt Tilly
Haslett's garden down by the creek the meadow larks
strutted in buff and yellow, with crescent-shaped gor-
gets of black at their throats, like Old Continentals,
sending their clear-piped warning of "Laziness g'wine
kill you!" in at the open windows of the steamy,
smelly courtroom.

The defense lost no time getting under headway.
As his main witness Durham called the prisoner to testify in his own behalf. Tandy gave his version of the
killing with a frankness and directness that would have
carried conviction to auditors more even-minded in
their sympathies. He had gone to Rankin's office in
the hope of bringing on a peaceful settlement of their
quarrel. Rankin had flared up; had cursed him and
advanced on him, making threats. Both of them
reached for their guns then. Rankin's was the first
out, but he fired first—that was all there was to it.
Gilliam shone at cross-examination; he went at Tandy

savagely, taking hold like a snapping turtle and hang-
ing on like one.

He made Tandy admit over and over again that
he carried a pistol habitually. In a community
where a third of the male adult population went armed
this admission was nevertheless taken as plain evidence of a nature bloody-minded and desperate. It
would have been just as bad for Tandy if he said he
armed himself especially for his visit to Rankin—
to these listeners that could have meant nothing else
but a deliberate, murderous intention. Either way
Gilliam had him, and he sweated in his eagerness to
bring out the significance of the point. A sinister
little murmuring sound, vibrant with menace, went
purring from bench to bench when Tandy told about
his pistol-carrying habit.

The cross-examination dragged along for hours. The
recess for dinner interrupted it; then it went on again,
Gilliam worrying at Tandy, goading at him, catching
him up and twisting his words. Tandy would not be
shaken, but twice under the manhandling he lost his
temper and lashed back at Gilliam, which was pre-
cisely what Gilliam most desired. A flary, fiery man,
prone to violent outbursts—that was the inference he
could draw from these blaze-ups.

It was getting on toward five o'clock before Gilliam
finally let his bedeviled enemy quit the witness-stand
and go back to his place between his wife and his
lawyer. As for Durham, he had little more to offer.
He called on Mr. Felsburg, and Mr. Felsburg gave
Tandy a good name as man and boy in his home town.
He called on Banker Quigley, who did the same thing
in different words. For these character witnesses
State's Attorney Gilliam had few questions. The case

was as good as won now, he figured; he could taste already his victory over the famous lawyer from up North, and he was greedy to hurry it forward.

The hot round hub of a sun had wheeled low enough to dart its thin red spokes in through the westerly windows when Durham called his last witness. As Judge Priest settled himself solidly in the witness chair with the deliberation of age and the heft of flesh, the leveled rays caught him full and lit up his round pink face, with the short white-bleached beard below it and the bald white-bleached forehead above. Durham eyed him half doubtfully. He looked the image of a scatter-witted old man, who would potter and philander round a long time before he ever came to the point of anything. So he appeared to the others there, too. But what Durham did not sense was that the homely simplicity of the old man was of a piece with the picture of the courtroom, that he would seem to these watching, hostile people one of their own kind, and that they would give to him in all likelihood a sympathy and understanding that had been denied the clothing merchant and the broadclothed banker.

He wore a black alpaca coat that slanted upon him in deep, longitudinal folds, and the front skirts of it were twisted and pulled downward until they dangled in long, wrinkly black teats. His shapeless gray trousers were short for him and fitted his pudgy legs closely. Below them dangled a pair of stout ankles encased in white cotton socks and ending in low-quarter black shoes. His shirt was clean but wrinkled countlessly over his front. The gnawed and blackened end of a cane pipestem stood out of his breast pocket, rising like a frosted weed stalk.

He settled himself back in the capacious oak chair,

balanced upon his knees a white straw hat with a string band round the crown and waited for the question.

"What is your name?" asked Durham.

"William Pitman Priest."

Even the voice somehow seemed to fit the setting. Its high nasal note had a sort of whimsical appeal to it.

"When and where were you born?"

"In Calloway County, Kintucky, July 27, 1839."

"What is your profession or business?"

"I am an attorney-at-law."

"What position if any do you hold in your native state?"

"I am presidin' judge of the first judicial district of the state of Kintucky."

"And have you been so long?"

"For the past sixteen years."

"When were you admitted to the bar?"

"In 1860."

"And you have ever since been engaged, I take it, either in the practise of the law before the bar or in its administration from the bench?"

"Exceptin' for the four years from April, 1861, to June, 1865."

Up until now Durham had been sparring, trying to fathom the probable trend of the old judge's expected meanderings. But in the answer to the last question he thought he caught the cue and, tho none save those two knew it, thereafter it was the witness who led and the questioner who followed his lead blindly.

"And where were you during those four years?"

"I was engaged, suh, in takin' part in the war."

"The War of the Rebellion?"

"No, suh," the old man corrected him gently but with firmness, "the War for the Southern Confederacy."

There was a least bit of a stir at this. Aunt Tilly's tape-edged palmleaf blade hovered a brief second in the wide regular arc of its sweep and the foreman of the jury involuntarily ducked his head, as if in affiance of an indubitable fact.

"Ahem!" said Durham, still feeling his way, altho now he saw the path more clearly. "And on which side were you engaged?"

"I was a private soldier in the Southern army," the old judge answered him, and as he spoke he straightened up.

"Yes, suh," he repeated, "for four years I was a private soldier in the late Southern Confederacy. Part of the time I was down here in this very country," he went on as tho he had just recalled that part of it. "Why, in the summer of '64 I was right here in this town. And until yistiddy I hadn't been back since."

He turned to the trial judge and spoke to him with a tone and manner half apologetic, half confidential.

"Your Honor," he said, "I am a judge myself, occupyin' in my home state a position very similar to the one which you fill here, and whilst I realize, none better, that this ain't all accordin' to the rules of evidence as laid down in the books, yet when I git to thinkin' about them old soldierin' times I find I am inclined to sort of reminiscence round a little. And I trust your Honor will pardon me if I should seem to ramble slightly?"

His tone was more than apologetic and more than confidential. It was winning. The judge upon the bench was a veteran himself. He looked toward the prosecutor.

"Has the state's attorney any objection to this line of testimony?" he asked, smiling a little.

Certainly Gilliam had no fear that this honest-appearing old man's wanderings could damage a case already as good as won. He smiled back indulgently and waved his arm with a gesture that was compounded of equal parts of toleration and patience, with a top-dressing of contempt. "I fail," said Gilliam, "to see wherein the military history and achievements of this worthy gentleman can possibly affect the issue of the homicide of Abner J. Rankin. But," he added magnanimously, "if the defense chooses to encumber the record with matters so trifling and irrelevant I surely will make no objection now or hereafter."

"The witness may proceed," said the judge.

"Well, really, Your Honor, I didn't have so very much to say," confessed Judge Priest, "and I didn't expect there'd be any to-do made over it. What I was trying to git at was that comin' down here to testify in this case sort of brought back them old days to my mind. As I git along more in years—" he was looking toward the jurors now—"I find that I live more and more in the past."

As tho he had put a question to them several of the jurors gravely inclined their heads. The busy cud of Juror No. 12 moved just a trifle slower in its travels from the right side of the jaw to the left and back again.

"Yes, suh," he said musingly, "I got up early this mornin' at the tavern where I'm stoppin' and took a walk through your thrivin' little city." This was rambling with a vengeance, thought the puzzled Durham. "I walked down here to a bridge over a little creek and back again. It reminded me mightily of that other time when I passed through this town—in '64— just about this season of the year—and it was hot early

today just as it was that other time—and the dew was
thick on the grass, the same as 'twas then."

He halted a moment.

"Of course your town didn't look the same this
mornin' as it did that other mornin'. It seemed like
to me there are twicet as many houses here now as
there used to be—it's got to be quite a little city."

Mr. Lukins, the grocer, nodded silent approval of
this utterance, Mr. Lukins having but newly completed
and moved into a two-story brick store building with
a tin cornice and an outside staircase.

"Yes, suh, your town has grown mightily, but"—
and the whiny, humorous voice grew apologetic again—
"but your roads are purty much the same as they
were in '64—hilly in places—and kind of rocky."

Durham found himself sitting still, listening hard.
Everybody else was listening too. Suddenly it struck
Durham, almost like a blow, that this simple old man
had somehow laid a sort of spell upon them all. The
flattening sunrays made a kind of pink glow about the
old judge's face, touching gently his bald head and his
white whiskers. He droned on:

"I remember about those roads particularly well,
because that time when I marched through here in '64
my feet was about out of my shoes and them flints
cut 'em up some. Some of the boys, I recollect, left
bloody prints in the dust behind 'em. But shucks—it
wouldn't a-made no real difference if we'd wore the
bottoms plum off our feet! We'd a-kept on goin'.
We'd a-gone anywhere—or tried to—behind old Bedford Forrest."

Aunt Tilly's palmleaf halted in air and the twelfth
juror's faithful quid froze in his cheek and stuck there
like a small wen. Except for a general hunching for-

ward of shoulders and heads there was no movement
anywhere and no sound except the voice of the witness:

"Old Bedford Forrest hisself was leadin' us, and
so naturally we just went along with him, shoes or no
shoes. There was a regiment of Northern troops—
Yankees—marchin' on this town that mornin', and it
seemed the word had traveled ahead of 'em that they
was aimin' to burn it down.

"Probably it wasn't true. When we got to know
them Yankees better afterward we found out that
there really wasn't no difference, to speak of, between
the run of us and the run of them. Probably it wasn't
so at all. But in them days the people were prone
to believe 'most anything—about Yankees—and the
word was that they was comin' across country, a-burn-
in' and cuttin' and slashin', and the people here
thought they was going to be burned out of house and
home. So old Bedford Forrest he marched all night
with a battalion of us—four companies—Kintuckians
and Tennesseeans mostly, with a sprinklin' of boys
from Mississippi and Arkansas—some of us ridin' and
some walkin' afoot, like me—we didn't always have
horses enough to go round that last year. And somehow we got here before they did. It was a close race
tho between us—them a-comin' down from the
North and us a-comin' up from the other way. We
met 'em down there by that little branch just below
where your present railroad depot is. There wasn't no
depot there then, but the branch looks just the same
now as it did then—and the bridge too. I walked
acros't it this mornin' to see. Yes, suh, right there
was where we met 'em. And there was a right smart
fight.

"Yes, suh, there was a right smart fight for about

twenty minutes—or maybe twenty-five—and then we had breakfast."

He had been smiling gently as he went along. Now he broke into a throaty little chuckle.

"Yes, suh, it all come back to me this mornin'—every little bit of it—the breakfast and all. I didn't have much breakfast, tho, as I recall—none of us did—probably just corn pone and branch water to wash it down with." And he wiped his mouth with the back of his hand as tho the taste of the gritty cornmeal cakes was still there.

There was another little pause here; the witness seemed to be through. Durham's crisp question cut the silence like a gash with a knife.

"Judge Priest, do you know the defendant at the bar, and if so, how well do you know him?"

"I was just comin' to that," he answered with simplicity, "and I'm obliged to you for puttin' me back on the track. Oh, I know the defendant at the bar mighty well—as well as anybody on earth ever did know him, I reckon, unless 'twas his own maw and paw. I've known him, in fact, from the time he was born—and a gentler, better-disposed boy never grew up in our town. His nature seemed almost too sweet for a boy—more like a girl's—but as a grown man he was always manly, and honest, and fair—and not quarrelsome. Oh, yes, I know him. I knew his father and his mother before him. It's a funny thing too—comin' up this way—but I remember that his paw was marchin' right alongside of me the day we came through here in '64. He was wounded, his paw was, right at the edge of that little creek down yonder. He was wounded in the shoulder—and he never did entirely git over it."

Again he stopped dead short, and he lifted his hand and tugged at the lobe of his right ear absently. Simultaneously Mr. Felsburg, who was sitting close to a window beyond the jury box, was also seized with nervousness, for he jerked out a handkerchief and with it mopped his brow so vigorously that, to one standing outside, it might have seemed that the handkerchief was actually being waved about as a signal.

Instantly then there broke upon the pause that still endured a sudden burst of music, a rollicking, jingling air. It was only a twenty-cent mouth organ, three sleigh bells, and a pair of rib bones of a beef-cow being played all at once by a saddle-colored negro man but it sounded for all the world like a fife-and-drum corps:

> *If you want to have a good time,*
> *If you want to have a good time,*
> *If you want to have a good time,*
> *If you want to ketch the devil—*
> *Jine the cavalree!*

To some who heard it now the tune was strange; these were the younger ones. But to those older men and the older women the first jubilant bars rolled back the years like a scroll.

> *If you want to have a good time,*
> *If you want to have a good time,*
> *If you want to have a good time,*
> *If you want to ride with Bedford—*
> *Jine the cavalree!*

The sound swelled and rippled and rose through the windows—the marching song of the Southern trooper—

Forrest's men, and Morgan's, and Jeb Stuart's and Joe Wheeler's. It had in it the jingle of saber chains, the creak of sweaty saddle-girths, the nimble clunk of hurrying hoofs. It had in it the clanging memories of a cause and a time that would live with these people as long as they lived and their children lived and their children's children. It had in it the one sure call to the emotions and the sentiments of these people.

And it rose and rose and then as the unseen minstrel went slouching down Main Street, toward the depot and the creek, it sank lower and became a thin thread of sound, and then a broken thread of sound, and then it died out altogether and once more there was silence in the courthouse of Forked Deer County.

Strangely enough not one listener had come to the windows to look out. The interruption from without had seemed part and parcel of what went on within. None faced to the rear, every one faced to the front.

There was Mr. Lukins now. As Mr. Lukins got upon his feet he said to himself in a tone of feeling that he be dad-fetched. But immediately changing his mind he stated that he would preferably be dad-blamed, and as he moved toward the bar rail one overhearing him might have gathered from remarks let fall that Mr. Lukins was going somewhere with the intention of being extensively dad-burned. But for all these threats Mr. Lukins didn't go anywhere, except as near the railing as he could press.

Nearly everybody else was standing up too. The state's attorney was on his feet with the rest, seemingly for the purpose of making some protest.

Had any one looked they might have seen that the ember in the smoldering eye of the old foreman had blazed up to a brown fire; that Juror No. 4, with

utter disregard for expense, was biting segments out of
the brim of his new brown-varnished straw hat; that
No. 7 had dropped his crutches on the floor, and that
no one, not even their owner, had heard them fall; that
all the jurors were half out of their chairs. But no
one saw these things, for at this moment there rose up
Aunt Tilly Haslett, a dominant figure, her huge wide
back blocking the view of three or four immediately
behind her.

Uncle Fayette laid a timid detaining hand upon
her and seemed to be saying something protestingly.

"Turn lose of me, Fate Haslett!" she commanded.
"Ain't you ashamed of yourse'f, to be tryin' to hold
me back when you know how my only dear brother
died a-followin' after Gineral Nathan Bedford Forrest.
Turn loose of me!"

She flirted her great arm and Uncle Fayette spun
flutteringly into the mass behind. The sheriff barred
her way at the gate of the bar.

"Mizz Haslett," he implored, "please, Mizz Haslett—
you must keep order in the cote."

Aunt Tilly halted in her onward move, head up high
and elbows out, and through her specs, blazing like
burning-glasses, she fixed on him a look that instantly
charred that unhappy official into a burning red ruin
of his own self-importance.

"Keep it yourse'f, High Sheriff Washington Nash,
Esquire," she bade him; "that's whut you git paid good
money for doin'. And git out of my way! I'm a-goin'
in there to that pore little lonesome thing settin' there
all by herself, and there ain't nobody goin' to hinder
me neither!"

The sheriff shrunk aside; perhaps it would be better
to say he evaporated aside. And public opinion, re-

organized and made over but still incarnate in Aunt Tilly Haslett, swept past the rail and settled like a billowing black cloud into a chair that the local attorney for the defense vacated just in time to save himself the inconvenience of having it snatched bodily from under him.

"There, honey," said Aunt Tilly crooningly as she gathered the forlorn little figure of the prisoner's wife in her arms like a child and mothered her up to her ample bombazined bosom, "there now, honey, you jest cry on me."

Then Aunt Tilly looked up and her specs were all blurry and wet. But she waved her palmleaf fan as tho it had been the baton of a marshal.

"Now, Jedge," she said, addressing the bench, "and you other gentlemen—you kin go ahead now."

The state's attorney had meant evidently to make some sort of an objection, for he was upon his feet through all this scene. But he looked back before he spoke and what he saw kept him from speaking. I believe I stated earlier that he was a candidate for reelection. So he settled back down in his chair and stretched out his legs and buried his chin in the top of his limp white waistcoat in an attitude that he had once seen in a picture entitled, "Napoleon Bonaparte at St. Helena."

"You may resume, Judge Priest," said the trial judge in a voice that was not entirely free from huskiness, altho its owner had been clearing it steadily for some moments.

"Thank you kindly, suh, but I was about through anyhow," answered the witness with a bow, and for all his homeliness there was dignity and stateliness in it. "I merely wanted to say for the sake of completin'

the record, so to speak, that on the occasion referred to
them Yankees did not cross that bridge."

With the air of tendering and receiving congratu-
lations Mr. Lukins turned to his nearest neighbor and
shook hands with him warmly.

The witness got up somewhat stiffly, once more
becoming a commonplace old man in a wrinkled black
alpaca coat, and made his way back to his vacant place,
now in the shadow of Aunt Tilly Haslett's form. As
he passed along the front of the jury-box the foreman's
crippled right hand came up in a sort of a clumsy
salute, and the juror at the other end of the rear
row—No. 12, the oldest juror—leaned forward as if
to speak to him, but remembered in time where his
present duty lay. The old judge kept on until he came
to Durham's side and he whispered to him:

"Son, they've quit lookin' at him and they're all
a-lookin' at her. Son, rest your case."

Durham came out of a maze.

"Your Honor," he said as he arose, "the defense
rests."

. . . .

The jury were out only six minutes. Mr. Lukins
insisted that it was only five minutes and a half, and
added that he'd be dad-rotted if it was a second longer
than that.

As the lately accused Tandy came out of the courthouse with his imported lawyer—Aunt Tilly bringing up the rear with his trembling, weeping, happy
little wife—friendly hands were outstretched to clasp
his and a whiskered old gentleman with a thumbnail
like a Brazil nut grabbed at his arm.

"Whichaway did Billy Priest go?" he demanded—

"little old Fightin' Billy—whar did he go to? Soon as he started in talkin' I placed him. Whar is he?"

Walking side by side, Tandy and Durham came down the steps into the soft June night, and Tandy took a long, deep breath into his lungs.

"Mr. Durham," he said, "I owe a great deal to you."

"How's that?" said Durham.

Just ahead of them, centered in a shaft of light from the window of the barroom of the Drummers' Home Hotel, stood Judge Priest. The old judge had been drinking. The pink of his face was a trifle more pronounced, the high whine in his voice a trifle weedier, as he counted one by one certain pieces of silver into a wide-open palm of a saddle-colored negro.

"How's that?" said Durham.

"I say I owe everything in the world to you," repeated Tandy.

"No," said Durham, "what you owe me is the fee you agreed to pay me for defending you. There's the man you're looking for."

And he pointed to the old judge.

HIS FIRST PENITENT

By James Oliver Curwood

Chapter I

In a white wilderness of moaning storm, in a wilderness of miles and miles of black pine-trees, the Transcontinental Flier lay buried in the snow.

In the first darkness of the wild December night, engine and tender had rushed on ahead to division headquarters, to let the line know that the flier had given up the fight, and needed assistance. They had been gone two hours, and whiter and whiter grew the brilliantly lighted coaches in the drifts and winnows of the whistling storm. From the black edges of the forest, prowling eyes might have looked upon scores of human faces staring anxiously out into the blackness from the windows of the coaches.

In those coaches it was growing steadily colder. Men were putting on their overcoats, and women snuggled deeper in their furs. Over it all, the tops of the black pine-trees moaned and whistled in sounds that seemed filled both with menace and with savage laughter.

In the smoking-compartment of the Pullman sat five men, gathered in a group. Of these, one was Forsythe, the timber agent; two were traveling men; the fourth a passenger homeward bound from a holiday visit; and the fifth was Father Charles.

All were smoking, and had been smoking for an hour, even to Father Charles, who lighted his third cigar as one of the traveling men finished the story he had been telling. They had passed away the tedious wait with tales of personal adventure and curious happenings. Each had furnished his share of entertainment, with the exception of Father Charles.

The priest's pale, serious face lit up in surprize or laughter with the others, but his lips had not broken into a story of their own. He was a little man, dressed in somber black, and there was that about him which told his companions that within his tight-drawn coat of shiny black there were hidden tales which would have gone well with the savage beat of the storm against lighted windows and the moaning tumult of the pine-trees.

Suddenly Forsythe shivered at a fiercer blast than the others, and said:

"Father, have you a text that would fit this night—and the situation?"

Slowly Father Charles blew out a spiral of smoke from between his lips, and then he drew himself erect and leaned a little forward, with the cigar between his slender white fingers.

"I had a text for this night," he said, "but I have none now, gentlemen. I was to have married a couple a hundred miles down the line. The guests have assembled. They are ready, but I am not there. The wedding will not be to-night, and so my text is gone. But there comes another to my mind which fits this situation—and a thousand others—'He who sits in the heavens shall look down and decide.' To-night I was to have married these young people. Three hours ago I never dreamed of doubting that I should be on

hand at the appointed hour. But I shall not marry
them. Fate has enjoined a hand. The Supreme Arbiter says 'No,' and what may not be the conse-
quences?"

"They will probably be married to-morrow," said
one of the traveling men. "There will be a few hours'
delay—nothing more."

"Perhaps," replied Father Charles, as quietly as before. "And—perhaps not. Who can say what this
little incident may not mean in the lives of that young
man and that young woman—and, it may be, in my
own? Three or four hours lost in a storm—what may
they not mean to more than one human heart on this
train? The Supreme Arbiter plays His hand, if you
wish to call it that, with reason and intent. To some
one, somewhere, the most insignificant occurrence may
mean life or death. And to-night—this—means something."

A sudden blast drove the night screeching over their
heads, and the wailing of the pines was almost human
voices. Forsythe sucked a cigar that had gone out.

"Long ago," said Father Charles, "I knew a young
man and a young woman who were to be married. The
man went West to win a fortune. Thus fate sep-
arated them, and in the lapse of a year such terrible
misfortune came to the girl's parents that she was
forced into a marriage with wealth—a barter of her
white body for an old man's gold. When the young
man returned from the West he found his sweetheart
married, and hell upon earth was their lot. But hope
lingers in young hearts. He waited four years; and
then, discouraged, he married another woman. Gentlemen, *three days* after the wedding his old sweetheart's
husband died, and she was released from bondage.

Was not that the hand of the Supreme Arbiter? If he had waited but three days more, the old happiness might have lived.

"But wait! One month after that day the young man was arrested, taken to a Western State, tried for murder, and hanged. Do you see the point? In three days more the girl who had sold herself into slavery for the salvation of those she loved would have been released from her bondage only to marry a murderer!"

Chapter II

There was a silence, in which all five listened to that wild moaning of the storm. There seemed to be something in it now—something more than the inarticulate sound of wind and trees. Forsythe scratched a match and relighted his cigar.

"I never thought of such things in just that light," he said.

"Listen to the wind," said the little priest. "Hear the pine-trees shriek out there! It recalls to me a night of years and years ago—a night like this, when the storm moaned and twisted about my little cabin, and when the Supreme Arbiter sent me my first penitent. Gentlemen, it is something which will bring you nearer to an understanding of the voice and the hand of God. It is a sermon on the mighty significance of little things, this story of my first penitent. If you wish, I will tell it to you."

"Go on," said Forsythe.

The traveling men drew nearer.

"It was a night like this," repeated Father Charles, "and it was in a great wilderness like this, only miles and miles away. I had been sent to establish a mission; and in my cabin, that wild night, alone and with the storm shrieking about me, I was busy at work sketching out my plans. After a time I grew nervous. I did not smoke then, and so I had nothing to comfort me but my thoughts; and, in spite of my efforts to make them otherwise, they were cheerless enough. The forest grew to my door. In the fiercer blasts I could hear the lashing of the pine-tops over my head, and now and then an arm of one of the moaning trees would reach down and sweep across my cabin roof with a sound that made me shudder and fear. This wilderness fear is an oppressive and terrible thing when you are alone at night, and the world is twisting and tearing itself outside. I have heard the pine-trees shriek like dying women, I have heard them wailing like lost children, I have heard them sobbing and moaning like human souls writhing in agony—"

Father Charles paused, to peer through the window out into the black night, where the pine-trees were sobbing and moaning now. When he turned, Forsythe, the timber agent, whose life was a wilderness life, nodded understandingly.

"And when they cry like that," went on Father Charles, "a living voice would be lost among them as the splash of a pebble is lost in a roaring sea. A hundred times that night I fancied that I heard human voices; and a dozen times I went to my door, drew back the bolt, and listened, with the snow and the wind beating about my ears.

"As I sat shuddering before my fire, there came a thought to me of a story which I had long ago read about the sea—a story of impossible achievement and of impossible heroism. As vividly as if I had read it only the day before, I recalled the description of a wild and stormy night when the heroine placed a lighted lamp in the window of her sea-bound cottage, to guide her lover home in safety. Gentlemen, the reading of that book in my boyhood days was but a trivial thing. I had read a thousand others, and of them all it was possibly the least significant; but the Supreme Arbiter had not forgotten.

"The memory of that book brought me to my feet, and I placed a lighted lamp close up against my cabin window. Fifteen minutes later I heard a strange sound at the door, and when I opened it there fell in upon the floor at my feet a young and beautiful woman. And after her, dragging himself over the threshold on his hands and knees, there came a man.

"I closed the door, after the man had crawled in and fallen face downward upon the floor, and turned my attention first to the woman. She was covered with snow. Her long, beautiful hair was loose and disheveled, and had blown about her like a veil. Her big, dark eyes looked at me pleadingly, and in them there was a terror such as I had never beheld in human eyes before. I bent over her, intending to carry her to my cot; but in another moment she had thrown herself upon the prostrate form of the man, with her arms about his head, and there burst from her lips the first sounds that she had uttered. They were not much more intelligible than the wailing grief of the pine-trees out in the night, but they told me plainly enough that the man on the floor was dearer to her than life.

"I knelt beside him, and found that he was breathing in a quick, panting sort of way, and that his wide-open eyes were looking at the woman. Then I noticed for the first time that his face was cut and bruised, and his lips were swollen. His coat was loose at the throat, and I could see livid marks on his neck.

"'I'm all right,' he whispered, struggling for breath, and turning his eyes to me. 'We should have died— in a few minutes more—if it hadn't been for the light in your window!'

"The young woman bent down and kissed him, and then she allowed me to help her to my cot. When I had attended to the young man, and he had regained strength enough to stand upon his feet, she was asleep. The man went to her, and dropped upon his knees beside the cot. Tenderly he drew back the heavy masses of hair from about her face and shoulders. For several minutes he remained with his face pressed close against hers; then he rose, and faced me. The woman—his wife—knew nothing of what passed between us during the next half-hour. During that half-hour, gentlemen, I received my first confession. The young man was of my faith. He was my first penitent."

It was growing colder in the coach, and Father Charles stopped to draw his thin black coat closer about him. Forsythe relighted his cigar for the third time. The transient passenger gave a sudden start as a gust of wind beat against the window like a threatening hand.

"A rough stool was my confessional, gentlemen," resumed Father Charles. "He told me the story, kneeling at my feet—a story that will live with me as long as I live, always reminding me that the little things of life may be the greatest things, that by sending a storm to hold up a coach the Supreme Arbiter